A
FLOWER FAIRIES
TREASURY

◆

A
FLOWER FAIRIES
TREASURY

PLANTAIN AND MOON-DAISY DANCING TOGETHER,
ALL THROUGH THE BEAUTIFUL SUNSHINY WEATHER

Poems and pictures by
CICELY MARY BARKER

◆

FREDERICK WARNE

The reproductions in this book have been made using the most modern electronic scanning methods from entirely new transparencies of Cicely Mary Barker's original watercolours. They enable her skill as an artist to be appreciated as never before.

The originals of some illustrations have been lost and so a first edition has been used to reproduce the following pictures: the Windflower Fairy, the Dandelion Fairy, the Daffodil Fairy, the Lady's Smock Fairy, the Stitchwort Fairy, the Daisy Fairy, the Dead-Nettle Fairy, the Celandine Fairy, the Dog-Violet Fairy, the Primrose Fairy, the Bluebell Fairy, the Speedwell Fairy, the Cowslip Fairy, the Heart's-Ease Fairy and the Snowdrop Fairy.

This edition published for Colour Library Books by
FREDERICK WARNE

Published by the Penguin Group
27 Wrights Lane, London W8 5TZ, England
Penguin Books USA Inc., 375 Hudson Street, New York, New York 10014, USA
Penguin Books Australia Ltd, Ringwood, Victoria, Australia
Penguin Books Canada Ltd, 10 Alcorn Avenue, Toronto, Ontario, Canada M4V 3B2
Penguin Books (NZ) Ltd, 182-190 Wairau Road, Auckland 10, New Zealand

Penguin Books Ltd, Registered Offices: Harmondsworth, Middlesex, England

This edition first published 1997 by Frederick Warne
1 3 5 7 9 10 8 6 4 2

This presentation copyright © The Estate of Cicely Mary Barker 1997
New reproductions of Cicely Mary Barker's illustrations copyright © The Estate of Cicely Mary Barker 1990
Text and illustrations copyright © The Estate of Cicely Mary Barker 1923, 1925, 1926, 1934, 1940, 1944, 1948

ISBN 0 7232 4409 X

Printed and bound in Singapore
by Tien Wah Press Ltd.

Contents

CONTENTS

◆

CONTENTS

◆

CONTENTS

◆

The Crocus Fairies

◆ THE SONG OF ◆
THE CROCUS FAIRIES

Crocus of yellow, new and gay;
Mauve and purple, in brave array;
    Crocus white
    Like a cup of light,—
Hundreds of them are smiling up,
Each with a flame in its shining cup,
By the touch of the warm and welcome sun
Opened suddenly. Spring's begun!
Dance then, fairies, for joy, and sing
The song of the coming again of Spring

◆ THE SONG OF ◆
THE WINDFLOWER FAIRY

While human-folk slumber,
  The fairies espy
Stars without number
  Sprinkling the sky.

The Winter's long sleeping,
  Like night-time, is done;
But day-stars are leaping
  To welcome the sun.

Star-like they sprinkle
  The wildwood with light;
Countless they twinkle—
  The Windflowers white!

("Windflower" is another name for Wood Anemone.)

16

The Windflower Fairy

The Dandelion Fairy

◆ THE SONG OF ◆
THE DANDELION FAIRY

Here's the Dandelion's rhyme:
   See my leaves with tooth-like edges;
Blow my clocks to tell the time;
   See me flaunting by the hedges,
In the meadow, in the lane,
   Gay and naughty in the garden;
Pull me up—I grow again,
   Asking neither leave nor pardon.
Sillies, what are you about
   With your spades and hoes of iron?
You can never drive me out—
   Me, the dauntless Dandelion!

◆ THE SONG OF ◆
THE DAFFODIL FAIRY

I'm everyone's darling: the blackbird and
    starling
Are shouting about me from blossoming
    boughs;
For I, the Lent Lily, the Daffy-down-dilly,
Have heard through the country the call to
    arouse.
The orchards are ringing with voices
    a-singing
The praise of my petticoat, praise of my
    gown;
The children are playing, and hark! they are
    saying
That Daffy-down-dilly is come up to town!

The Daffodil Fairy

The Lady's-Smock Fairy

◆ THE SONG OF ◆
THE LADY'S-SMOCK FAIRY

Where the grass is damp and green,
Where the shallow streams are flowing,
Where the cowslip buds are showing,
    I am seen.

Dainty as a fairy's frock,
White or mauve, of elfin sewing,
'Tis the meadow-maiden growing—
    Lady's-smock.

◆ THE SONG OF ◆
THE STITCHWORT FAIRY

I am brittle-stemmed and slender,
But the grass is my defender.

On the banks where grass is long,
I can stand erect and strong.

All my mass of starry faces
Looking up from wayside places,

From the thick and tangled grass,
Gives you greeting as you pass.

(A prettier name for Stitchwort is Starwort, but it is not
so often used.)

The Stitchwort Fairy

The Daisy Fairy.

The Daisy Fairy

◆ THE SONG OF ◆
THE DAISY FAIRY

Come to me and play with me,
  I'm the babies' flower;
Make a necklace gay with me,
Spend the whole long day with me,
  Till the sunset hour.

I must say Good-night, you know,
  Till tomorrow's playtime;
Close my petals tight, you know,
Shut the red and white, you know,
  Sleeping till the daytime.

◆ THE SONG OF ◆
THE BUTTERCUP FAIRY

'Tis I whom children love the best;
　　My wealth is all for them;
For them is set each glossy cup
　　Upon each sturdy stem.

O little playmates whom I love!
　　The sky is summer-blue,
And meadows full of buttercups
　　Are spread abroad for you.

The Buttercup Fairy

The Forget-me-not Fairy

◆ THE SONG OF ◆
THE FORGET-ME-NOT FAIRY

So small, so blue, in grassy places
    My flowers raise
    Their tiny faces.

By streams my bigger sisters grow,
    And smile in gardens,
    In a row.

I've never seen a garden plot;
    But though I'm small
    Forget me not!

◆ THE SONG OF ◆
THE FOXGLOVE FAIRY

"Foxglove, Foxglove,
　What do you see?"
The cool green woodland,
　The fat velvet bee;
Hey, Mr Bumble,
　I've honey here for thee!

"Foxglove, Foxglove,
　What see you now?"
The soft summer moonlight
　On bracken, grass, and bough;
And all the fairies dancing
　As only they know how.

The Foxglove Fairy

The Wild Rose Fairy

◆ THE SONG OF ◆
THE WILD ROSE FAIRY

I am the queen whom everybody knows:
    I am the English Rose;
As light and free as any Jenny Wren,
    As dear to Englishmen;
As joyous as a Robin Redbreast's tune,
    I scent the air of June;
My buds are rosy as a baby's cheek;
    I have one word to speak,
One word which is my secret and my song,
'Tis "England, England, England" all day long.

◆ THE SONG OF ◆
THE HAREBELL FAIRY

O bells, on stems so thin and fine!
    No human ear
    Your sound can hear,
O lightly chiming bells of mine!

When dim and dewy twilight falls,
    Then comes the time
    When harebells chime
For fairy feasts and fairy balls.

They tinkle while the fairies play,
    With dance and song,
    The whole night long,
Till daybreak wakens, cold and grey,
And elfin music fades away.

(The Harebell is the Bluebell of Scotland.)

The Harebell Fairy

The Toadflax Fairy

◆ THE SONG OF ◆
THE TOADFLAX FAIRY

The children, the children,
      they call me funny names,
They take me for their darling
      and partner in their games;
They pinch my flowers' yellow mouths,
      to open them and close,
Saying, *Snap-Dragon!*
            Toadflax!
                  or, *darling Bunny-Nose!*

The Toadflax, the Toadflax,
      with lemon-coloured spikes,
With funny friendly faces
      that everybody likes,
Upon the grassy hillside
      and hedgerow bank it grows,
And it's *Snap-Dragon !*
            Toadflax!
                  and *darling Bunny-Nose!*

◆ THE SONG OF ◆
THE SCABIOUS FAIRY

Like frilly cushions full of pins
For tiny dames and fairykins;

Or else like dancers decked with gems,
My flowers sway on slender stems.

They curtsey in the meadow grass,
And nod to butterflies who pass.

The Scabious Fairy

The Traveller's Joy Fairy

◆ THE SONG OF ◆
THE TRAVELLER'S JOY FAIRY

Traveller, traveller, tramping by
To the seaport town where the big ships lie,
See, I have built a shady bower
To shelter you from the sun or shower.
Rest for a bit, then on, my boy!
Luck go with you, and Traveller's Joy!

Traveller, traveller, tramping home
From foreign places beyond the foam,
See, I have hung out a white festoon
To greet the lad with the dusty shoon.
Somewhere a lass looks out for a boy:
Luck be with you, and Traveller's Joy!

(Traveller's Joy is Wild Clematis; and when the flowers are
over, it becomes a mass of silky fluff, and then we call it Old-
Man's-Beard.)

◆ THE SONG OF ◆
THE MOUNTAIN ASH FAIRY

They thought me, once, a magic tree
   Of wondrous lucky charm,
And at the door they planted me
   To keep the house from harm.

They have no fear of witchcraft now,
   Yet here am I today;
I've hung my berries from the bough,
   And merrily I say:

"Come, all you blackbirds, bring your wives,
   Your sons and daughters too;
The finest banquet of your lives
   Is here prepared for you."

(The Mountain Ash's other name is Rowan; and it used to
be called Witchentree and Witch-wood too.)

The Mountain Ash Fairy

The Horse Chestnut Fairy

◆ THE SONG OF ◆
THE HORSE CHESTNUT FAIRY

My conkers, they are shiny things,
   And things of mighty joy,
And they are like the wealth of kings
   To every little boy;
I see the upturned face of each
   Who stands around the tree:
He sees his treasure out of reach,
   But does not notice *me*.

For love of conkers bright and brown,
   He pelts the tree all day;
With stones and sticks he knocks them down,
   And thinks it jolly play.
But sometimes I, the elf, am hit
   Until I'm black and blue;
O laddies, only wait a bit,
   I'll shake them down to you!

◆ THE SONG OF ◆
THE NIGHTSHADE BERRY FAIRY

"You see my berries, how they gleam and
      glow,
Clear ruby-red, and green, and orange-
      yellow;
Do they not tempt you, fairies, dangling so?"
   The fairies shake their heads and answer "No!
     You are a crafty fellow!"

"What, won't you try them? There is
      naught to pay!
Why should you think my berries poisoned
      things?
You fairies may look scared and fly away—
The children will believe me when I say
     My fruit is fruit for kings!"
   But all good fairies cry in anxious haste,
"O children, do not taste!"

(You must believe the good fairies, though the berries look
nice. This is the Woody Nightshade, which has purple and
yellow flowers in the summer.)

The Nightshade Berry Fairy

The Crab-Apple Fairy

◆ THE SONG OF ◆
THE CRAB-APPLE FAIRY

Crab-apples, Crab-apples, out in the wood,
Little and bitter, yet little and good!
The apples in orchards, so rosy and fine,
Are children of wild little apples like mine.

The branches are laden, and droop to the
     ground;
The fairy-fruit falls in a circle around;
Now all you good children, come gather
     them up:
They'll make you sweet jelly to spread
     when you sup.

One little apple I'll catch for myself;
I'll stew it, and strain it, to store on a shelf
In four or five acorn-cups, locked with a key
In a cupboard of mine at the root of the tree.

◆ THE SONG OF ◆
THE HAZEL-NUT FAIRY

Slowly, slowly, growing
   While I watched them well,
See, my nuts have ripened;
   Now I've news to tell.
I will tell the Squirrel,
   "Here's a store for you;
But, kind Sir, remember
   The Nuthatch likes them too."

I will tell the Nuthatch,
   "Now, Sir, you may come;
Choose your nuts and crack them,
   But leave the children some."
I will tell the children,
   "You may take your share;
Come and fill your pockets,
   But leave a few to spare."

The Hazel-Nut Fairy

The Hawthorn Fairy

◆ THE SONG OF ◆
THE HAWTHORN FAIRY

These thorny branches bore the May
 So many months ago,
That when the scattered petals lay
 Like drifts of fallen snow,
  "This is the story's end," you said;
  But O, not half was told!
For see, my haws are here instead,
And hungry birdies shall be fed
 On these when days are cold.

◆ THE SONG OF ◆
THE SLOE FAIRY

When Blackthorn blossoms leap to sight,
They deck the hedge with starry light,
        In early Spring
        When rough winds blow,
        Each promising
        A purple sloe.

And now is Autumn here, and lo,
The Blackthorn bears the purple sloe!
        But ah, how much
        Too sharp these plums,
        Until the touch
        Of Winter comes!

(The sloe is a wild plum. One bite will set your teeth on
edge until it has been mellowed by frost; but it is not poisonous.)

The Sloe Fairy

The Yew Fairy

◆ THE SONG OF ◆
THE YEW FAIRY

Here, on the dark and solemn Yew,
   A marvel may be seen,
Where waxen berries, pink and new,
   Appear amid the green.

I sit a-dreaming in the tree,
   So old and yet so new;
One hundred years, or two, or three
   Are little to the Yew.

I think of bygone centuries,
   And seem to see anew
The archers face their enemies
   With bended bows of Yew.

◆ THE SONG OF ◆
THE WINTER JASMINE FAIRY

All through the Summer my leaves were green,
But never a flower of mine was seen;
Now Summer is gone, that was so gay,
And my little green leaves are shed away.
  In the grey of the year
  What cheer, what cheer?

The Winter is come, the cold winds blow;
I shall feel the frost and the drifting snow;
But the sun can shine in December too,
And this is the time of my gift to you.
  See here, see here,
  My flowers appear!

The swallows have flown beyond the sea,
But friendly Robin, he stays with me;
And little Tom-Tit, so busy and small,
Hops where the jasmine is thick on the wall;
  And we say: "Good cheer!
  We're here! We're here!"

The Winter Jasmine Fairy

The Dead-Nettle Fairy

◆ THE SONG OF ◆
THE DEAD-NETTLE FAIRY

Through sun and rain, the country lane,
The field, the road, are my abode.
Though leaf and bud be splashed with mud,
Who cares? Not I!—I see the sky,
The kindly sun, the wayside fun
Of tramping folk who smoke and joke,
The bairns who heed my dusty weed
(No sting have I to make them cry),
And truth to tell, they love me well.
My brothers, White, and Yellow bright,
Are finer chaps than I, perhaps;
Who cares? Not I! So now good-bye.

◆ THE SONG OF ◆
THE RUSH-GRASS AND
COTTON-GRASS FAIRIES

Safe across the moorland
 Travellers may go,
If they heed our warning—
 We're the ones who know!

Let the footpath guide you—
 You'll be safely led;
There is bog beside you
 Where you cannot tread!

Mind where you are going!
 If you turn aside
Where you see us growing,
 Trouble will betide.

Keep you to the path, then!
 Hark to what we say!
Else, into the quagmire
 You will surely stray.

The Rush-Grass and
Cotton-Grass Fairies

The Lords-and-Ladies Fairy

◆ THE SONG OF ◆
THE LORDS-AND-LADIES FAIRY

Fairies, when you lose your way,
   From the dance returning,
In the darkest undergrowth
   See my candles burning!
These shall make the pathway plain
Homeward to your beds again.

(These are the berries of the Wild Arum, which has many
other names, and has a flower like a hood in the Spring.
The berries are not to be eaten.)

◆ THE SONG OF ◆
THE PINE TREE FAIRY

A tall, tall tree is the Pine tree,
    With its trunk of bright red-brown—
The red of the merry squirrels
    Who go scampering up and down.

There are cones on the tall, tall Pine tree,
    With its needles sharp and green;
Small seeds in the cones are hidden,
    And they ripen there unseen.

The elves play games with the squirrels
    At the top of the tall, tall tree,
Throwing cones for the squirrels to nibble—
    I wish I were there to see!

The Pine Tree Fairy

The Holly Fairy

◆ THE SONG OF ◆
THE HOLLY FAIRY

O, I am green in Winter-time,
  When other trees are brown;
Of all the trees (So saith the rhyme)
  The holly bears the crown.
December days are drawing near
  When I shall come to town,
And carol-boys go singing clear
Of all the trees (O hush and hear!)
  The holly bears the crown!

For who so well-beloved and merry
As the scarlet Holly Berry?

◆ THE SONG OF ◆
THE WILD CHERRY BLOSSOM

In April when the woodland ways
    Are all made glad and sweet
With primroses and violets
    New-opened at your feet,
        Look up and see
            A fairy tree,
        With blossoms white
            In clusters light,
All set on stalks so slender,
    With pinky leaves so tender.
O Cherry tree, wild Cherry tree!
    You lovely, lovely thing to see!

The Wild Cherry Blossom Fairy

The Laburnum Fairy

◆ THE SONG OF ◆
THE LABURNUM FAIRY

All Laburnum's
Yellow flowers
Hanging thick
In happy showers,—
Look at them!
The reason's plain
Why folks call them
"Golden Rain"!
"Golden Chains"
They call them too,
Swinging there
Against the blue.

(After the flowers, the Laburnum has pods with what look
like tiny green peas in them; but it is best not to play with
them, and they must never, never be eaten, as they are
poisonous.)

◆ THE SONG OF ◆
THE SYCAMORE FAIRY

Because my seeds have wings, you know,
  They fly away to earth;
And where they fall, why, there they grow—
  New Sycamores have birth!
Perhaps a score? Oh, hundreds more!
  Too many, people say!
And yet to me it's fun to see
  My winged seeds fly away.
(But first they must turn ripe and brown,
  And lose their flush of red;
And *then* they'll all go twirling down
  To earth, to find a bed.)

The Sycamore Fairy

The Lime Tree Fairy

◆ THE SONG OF ◆
THE LIME TREE FAIRY

Bees! bees! come to the trees
Where the Lime has hung her treasures;
Come, come, hover and hum;
Come and enjoy your pleasures!
The feast is ready, the guests are bidden;
Under the petals the honey is hidden;
Like pearls shine the drops of sweetness there,
And the scent of the Lime-flowers fills the air.
But soon these blossoms pretty and pale
Will all be gone; and the leaf-like sail
Will bear the little round fruits away;
So bees! bees! come while you may!

◆ THE SONG OF ◆
THE MULBERRY FAIRY

"Here we go round the Mulberry bush!"
You remember the rhyme—oh yes!
But which of you know
How Mulberries grow
On the slender branches, drooping low?
Not many of you, I guess.

Someone goes round the Mulberry bush
When nobody's there to see;
He takes the best
And he leaves the rest,
From top to toe like a Mulberry drest:
This fat little fairy's he!

The Mulberry Fairy

The Willow Fairy

◆ THE SONG OF ◆
THE WILLOW FAIRY

By the peaceful stream or the shady pool
I dip my leaves in the water cool.

Over the water I lean all day,
Where the sticklebacks and the minnows play.

I dance, I dance, when the breezes blow,
And dip my toes in the stream below.

◆ THE SONG OF ◆
THE ALDER FAIRY

By the lake or river-side
    Where the Alders dwell,
In the Autumn may be spied
    Baby catkins; cones beside—
Old and new as well.
    Seasons come and seasons go;
That's the tale they tell!

After Autumn, Winter's cold
    Leads us to the Spring;
And, before the leaves unfold,
On the Alder you'll behold,
    Crimson catkins swing!
They are making ready now:
    That's the song I sing!

The Alder Fairy

The Silver Birch Fairy

◆ THE SONG OF ◆
THE SILVER BIRCH FAIRY

There's a gentle tree with a satiny bark,
All silver-white, and upon it, dark,
Is many a crosswise line and mark—
    She's a tree there's no mistaking!
The Birch is this light and lovely tree,
And as light and lovely still is she
When the Summer's time has come to flee,
    As she was at Spring's awaking.

She has new Birch-catkins, small and tight,
Though the old ones scatter
   and take their flight,
And the little leaves, all yellow and bright,
    In the autumn winds are shaking.
And with fluttering wings
   and hands that cling,
The fairies play and the fairies swing
On the fine thin twigs,
   that will toss and spring
    With never a fear of breaking.

◆ THE SONG OF ◆
THE NARCISSUS FAIRY

Brown bulbs were buried deep;
Now, from the kind old earth,
Out of the winter's sleep,
   Comes a new birth!

Flowers on stems that sway;
Flowers of snowy white;
Flowers as sweet as day,
   After the night.

So does Narcissus bring
Tidings most glad and plain:
"Winter's gone; here is Spring—
   Easter again!"

The Narcissus Fairy

The Cornflower Fairy

◆ THE SONG OF ◆
THE CORNFLOWER FAIRY

'Mid scarlet of poppies and gold of the corn,
In wide-spreading fields were the Cornflowers born;
But now I look round me, and what do I see?
That lilies and roses are neighbours to me!
There's a beautiful lawn, there are borders and beds,
Where all kinds of flowers raise delicate heads;
For this is a garden, and here, a Boy Blue,
I live and am merry the whole summer through.
My blue is the blue that I always have worn,
And still I remember the poppies and corn.

◆ THE SONG OF ◆
THE GERANIUM FAIRY

Red, red, vermilion red,
With buds and blooms in a glorious head!
There isn't a flower, the wide world through,
That glows with a brighter scarlet hue.
Her name—Geranium—ev'ryone knows;
She's just as happy wherever she grows,
In an earthen pot or a garden bed—
Red, red, vermilion red!

The Geranium Fairy

The Canterbury Bell Fairy

◆ THE SONG OF ◆
THE CANTERBURY BELL FAIRY

Bells that ring from ancient towers—
    Canterbury Bells—
Give their name to summer flowers—
    Canterbury Bells!
Do the flower-fairies, playing,
Know what those great bells are saying?
    Fairy, in your purple hat,
    Little fairy, tell us that!

"Naught I know of bells in towers—
    Canterbury Bells!
Mine are pink or purple flowers—
    Canterbury Bells!
When I set them all a-swaying,
Something, too, my bells are saying;
Can't you hear them—*ding-dong-ding*—
    Calling fairy-folk to sing?"

◆ THE SONG OF ◆
THE SHIRLEY POPPY FAIRY

We were all of us scarlet, and counted as
    weeds,
  When we grew in the fields with the corn;
Now, fall from your pepper-pots, wee little
    seeds,
  And lovelier things shall be born!

You shall sleep in the soil, and awaken next
    year;
  Your buds shall burst open; behold!
Soft-tinted and silken, shall petals appear,
  And then into Poppies unfold—

Like daintiest ladies, who dance and are gay,
  All frilly and pretty to see!
So I shake out the ripe little seeds, and I say:
  "Go, sleep, and awaken like me!"

(A clergyman, who was also a clever gardener, made these
many-coloured poppies out of the wild ones, and named them
after the village where he was the Vicar.)

The Shirley Poppy Fairy

The Candytuft Fairy

◆ THE SONG OF ◆
THE CANDYTUFT FAIRY

Why am I "Candytuft"?
That I don't know!
Maybe the fairies
First called me so;
Maybe the children,
Just for a joke;
(I'm in the gardens
Of most little folk).

Look at my clusters!
See how they grow:
Some pink or purple,
Some white as snow;
Petals uneven,
Big ones and small;
Not very tufty—
No candy at all!

◆ THE SONG OF ◆
THE GAILLARDIA FAIRY

There once was a child in a garden,
   Who loved all my colours of flame,
The crimson and scarlet and yellow—
   But what was my name?

For *Gaillardia*'s hard to remember!
   She looked at my yellow and red,
And thought of the gold and the glory
   When the sun goes to bed;

And she troubled no more to remember,
   But gave me a splendid new name;
She spoke of my flowers as *Sunsets*—
   Then *you* do the same!

The Gaillardia Fairy

The Sweet Pea Fairies

◆ THE SONG OF ◆
THE SWEET PEA FAIRIES

Here Sweet Peas are climbing;
  (Here's the Sweet Pea rhyme!)
Here are little tendrils,
  Helping them to climb.

Here are sweetest colours;
  Fragrance very sweet;
Here are silky pods of peas,
  Not for us to eat!

Here's a fairy sister,
  Trying on with care
Such a grand new bonnet
  For the baby there.

Does it suit you, Baby?
  Yes, I really think
Nothing's more becoming
  Than this pretty pink!

◆ THE SONG OF ◆
THE JACK-BY-THE-HEDGE FAIRY

"'Morning, Sir, and how-d'ye-do?
  'Morning, pretty lady!"
That is Jack saluting you,
  Where the lane is shady.

Don't you know him? Straight and tall—
  Taller than the nettles;
Large and light his leaves; and small
  Are his buds and petals.

Small and white, with petals four,
  See his flowers growing!
If you never knew before,
  There is Jack for knowing!

(Jack-by-the-hedge is also called Garlic Mustard, and
Sauce Alone.)

The Jack-by-the-hedge Fairy

The Ground Ivy Fairy

◆ THE SONG OF ◆
THE GROUND IVY FAIRY

In Spring he is found;
He creeps on the ground;
But someone's to blame
For the rest of his name—
For Ivy he's *not*!
Oh dear, what a lot
Of muddles we make!
It's quite a mistake,
And really a pity
Because he's so pretty;
He deserves a nice name—
Yes, *someone's* to blame!

(But he has some other names, which we do not hear very
often; here are four of them: Robin-run-up-the-dyke,
Runnadyke, Run-away-Jack, Creeping Charlie.)

◆ THE SONG OF ◆
THE BLACK MEDICK FAIRIES

"Why are we called 'Black', sister,
  When we've yellow flowers?"
"I will show you why, brother:
  See these seeds of ours?
Very soon each tiny seed
  Will be turning black indeed!"

The Black Medick Fairies

The Ribwort Plantain Fairy

◆ THE SONG OF ◆
THE RIBWORT PLANTAIN FAIRY

Hullo, Snailey-O!
How's the world with *you*?
Put your little horns out;
Tell me how you do?
There's rain, and dust, and sunshine,
Where carts go creaking by;
You like it wet, Snailey;
I like it dry!

Hey ho, Snailey-O,
I'll whistle you a tune!
I'm merry in September
As e'er I am in June.
By any stony roadside
Wherever you may roam,
All the summer through, Snailey,
Plantain's at home!

(There are some other kinds of Plantain besides this. The
one with wide leaves, and tall spikes of seed which canaries
enjoy, is Greater Plantain.)

◆ THE SONG OF ◆
THE FUMITORY FAIRY

Given me hundreds of years ago,
My name has a meaning you shall know:
It means, in the speech of the bygone folk,
"Smoke of the Earth" —a soft green smoke!

A wonderful plant to them I seemed;
Strange indeed were the dreams they dreamed,
Partly fancy and partly true,
About "Fumiter" and the way it grew.

Where men have ploughed
    or have dug the ground,
Still, with my rosy flowers, I'm found;
Known and prized by the bygone folk
As "Smoke of the Earth" —
    a soft green smoke!

(The name "Fumitory" was "Fumiter" 300 years ago;
and long before that, "Fume Terre", which is the French
name, still, for the plant. "Fume" means "smoke", "terre"
means "earth".)

The Fumitory Fairy

The Chicory Fairy

◆ THE SONG OF ◆
THE CHICORY FAIRY

By the white cart-road,
   Dusty and dry,
Look! there is Chicory,
   Blue as the sky!

Or, where the footpath
   Goes through the corn,
See her bright flowers,
   Each one new-born!

Though they fade quickly,
   O, have no sorrow!
There will be others
   New-born tomorrow!

(Chicory is also called Succory.)

◆ THE SONG OF ◆
THE JACK-GO-TO-BED-
AT-NOON FAIRY

I'll be asleep by noon!
Though bedtime comes so soon,
   I'm busy too.
Twelve puffs!—and then from sight
I shut my flowers tight;
Only by morning light
   They're seen by you.

Then, on some day of sun,
They'll open wide, each one,
   As something new!
Shepherd, who minds his flock,
Calls it a Shepherd's Clock,
Though it can't say "tick-tock"
   As others do!

(Another of Jack's names, besides Shepherd's Clock is
Goat's Beard.)

The Jack-go-to-bed-at-noon Fairy

The White Bindweed Fairy

◆ THE SONG OF ◆
THE WHITE BINDWEED FAIRY

O long long stems that twine!
O buds, so neatly furled!
O great white bells of mine,
(None purer in the world)
Each lasting but one day!
O leafy garlands, hung
In wreaths beside the way—
Well may your praise be sung!

(But this Bindweed, which is a big sister to the little pink
Field Convolvulus, is not good to have in gardens, though it is
so beautiful; because it winds around other plants and trees.
One of its names is "Hedge Strangler". Morning Glories are
a garden kind of Convolvulus.)

◆ THE SONG OF ◆
THE APPLE BLOSSOM FAIRIES

Up in the tree we see you, blossom-babies,
　　All pink and white;
We think there must be fairies to protect you
　　From frost and blight,
Until, some windy day, in drifts of petals,
　　You take your flight.

You'll fly away! But if we wait with patience,
　　Some day we'll find
Here, in your place, full-grown and ripe, the apples
　　You left behind—
A goodly gift indeed, from blossom-babies
　　To human-kind!

Apple Blossom

The Apple Blossom Fairies

Fuchsia

The Fuchsia Fairy

◆ THE SONG OF ◆
THE FUCHSIA FAIRY

Fuchsia is a dancer
Dancing on her toes,
Clad in red and purple,
By a cottage wall;
Sometimes in a greenhouse,
In frilly white and rose,
Dressed in her best for the fairies' evening ball!

(This is the little out-door Fuchsia.)

◆ THE SONG OF ◆
THE IRIS FAIRY

I am Iris: I'm the daughter
Of the marshland and the water.
Looking down, I see the gleam
Of the clear and peaceful stream;
Water-lilies large and fair
With their leaves are floating there;
All the water-world I see,
And my own face smiles at me!

(This is the wild Iris.)

Iris

The Iris Fairy

Jasmine

The Jasmine Fairy

◆ THE SONG OF ◆
THE JASMINE FAIRY

In heat of summer days
With sunshine all ablaze,
Here, here are cool green bowers,
Starry with Jasmine flowers;
Sweet-scented, like a dream
Of Fairyland they seem.

And when the long hot day
At length has worn away,
And twilight deepens, till
The darkness comes—then, still,
The glimmering Jasmine white
Gives fragrance to the night.

◆ THE SONG OF ◆
THE NASTURTIUM FAIRY

Nasturtium the jolly,
  O ho, O ho!
He holds up his brolly
  Just so, just so!
(A shelter from showers,
  A shade from the sun;)
'Mid flame-coloured flowers
  He grins at the fun.
Up fences he scrambles,
  Sing hey, sing hey!
All summer he rambles
  So gay, so gay—
Till the night-frost strikes chilly,
  And Autumn leaves fall,
And he's gone, willy-nilly,
  Umbrella and all.

N

Nasturtium

The Nasturtium Fairy

Pansy

The Pansy Fairy

◆ THE SONG OF ◆
THE PANSY FAIRY

Pansy and Petunia,
Periwinkle, Pink—
How to choose the best of them,
Leaving out the rest of them,
   That is hard, I think.

Poppy with its pepper-pots,
Polyanthus, Pea—
Though I wouldn't slight the rest,
Isn't Pansy *quite* the best,
   Quite the best for P?

Black and brown and velvety,
Purple, yellow, red;
Loved by people big and small,
All who plant and dig at all
   In a garden bed.

131

◆ THE SONG OF ◆
THE RAGGED ROBIN FAIRY

In wet marshy meadows
A tattered piper strays—
Ragged, ragged Robin;
On thin reeds he plays.

He asks for no payment;
He plays, for delight,
A tune for the fairies
To dance to, at night.

They nod and they whisper,
And say, looking wise,
"A princeling is Robin,
For all his disguise!

Ragged Robin

The Ragged Robin Fairy

The
Celandine
Fairy.

The Celandine Fairy

◆ THE SONG OF ◆
THE CELANDINE FAIRY

Before the hawthorn leaves unfold,
Or buttercups put forth their gold,
By every sunny footpath shine
The stars of Lesser Celandine.

◆ THE SONG OF ◆
THE DOG-VIOLET FAIRY

The wren and robin hop around;
   The Primrose-maids my neighbours be;
The sun has warmed the mossy ground;
Where Spring has come, I too am found:
   The Cuckoo's call has wakened me!

The Dog-Violet Fairy

The Primrose Fairy.

The Primrose Fairy

◆ THE SONG OF ◆
THE PRIMROSE FAIRY

The Primrose opens wide in spring;
　　Her scent is sweet and good:
It smells of every happy thing
　　In sunny lane and wood.
I have not half the skill to sing
　　And praise her as I should.

She's dear to folk throughout the land;
　　In her is nothing mean:
She freely spreads on every hand
　　Her petals pale and clean.
And though she's neither proud nor grand,
　　She is the Country Queen.

◆ THE SONG OF ◆
THE BLUEBELL FAIRY

My hundred thousand bells of blue,
   The splendour of the Spring,
They carpet all the woods anew
With royalty of sapphire hue;
The Primrose is the Queen, 'tis true.
   But surely I am King!
      Ah yes,
   The peerless Woodland King!

Loud, loud the thrushes sing their song;
   The bluebell woods are wide;
My stems are tall and straight and strong;
From ugly streets the children throng,
They gather armfuls, great and long,
   Then home they troop in pride—
      Ah yes,
   With laughter and with pride!

(This is the Wild Hyacinth. The Bluebell of Scotland
is the Harebell.)

The Bluebell Fairy

The Speedwell Fairy

◆ THE SONG OF ◆
THE SPEEDWELL FAIRY

Clear blue are the skies;
  My petals are blue;
  As beautiful, too,
As bluest of eyes.

The heavens are high:
  By the field-path I grow
  Where wayfarers go,
And "Good speed," say I;

"See, here is a prize
  Of wonderful worth:
  A weed of the earth,
As blue as the skies!"

(There are many kinds of Speedwell: this is the Germander.)

◆ THE SONG OF ◆
THE COWSLIP FAIRY

The land is full of happy birds
And flocks of sheep and grazing herds.

I hear the songs of larks that fly
Above me in the breezy sky.

I hear the little lambkins bleat;
My honey-scent is rich and sweet.

Beneath the sun I dance and play
In April and in merry May.

The grass is green as green can be;
The children shout at sight of me.

The Cowslip Fairy

The Heart's-Ease Fairy

◆ THE SONG OF ◆
THE HEART'S-EASE FAIRY

Like the richest velvet
　　(I've heard the fairies tell)
Grow the handsome pansies
　　within the garden wall;
When you praise their beauty,
　　remember me as well—
Think of little Heart's-ease,
　　the brother of them all!

Come away and seek me
　　when the year is young,
Through the open ploughlands
　　beyond the garden wall;
Many names are pretty
　　and many songs are sung:
Mine—because I'm Heart's-ease—
　　are prettiest of all!

(An old lady says that when she was a little girl the children's
name for the Heart's-ease or Wild Pansy was Jump-up-and-
kiss-me!)

147

◆ THE SONG OF ◆
THE POPPY FAIRY

The green wheat's a-growing,
　The lark sings on high;
In scarlet silk a-glowing,
　Here stand I.

The wheat's turning yellow,
　Ripening for sheaves;
I hear the little fellow
　Who scares the bird-thieves.

Now the harvest's ended,
　The wheat-field is bare;
But still, red and splendid,
　I am there.

The Poppy Fairy

The Bird's-Foot Trefoil Fairy

◆ THE SONG OF ◆
THE BIRD'S-FOOT TREFOIL FAIRY

Here I dance in a dress like flames,
And laugh to think of my comical names.
Hoppetty hop, with nimble legs!
Some folks call me *Bacon and Eggs*!
While other people, it's really true,
Tell me I'm *Cuckoo's Stockings* too!
Over the hill I skip and prance;
I'm *Lady's Slipper,* and so I dance,
Not like a lady, grand and proud,
But to the grasshoppers' chirping loud.
My pods are shaped like a dicky's toes:
That is what *Bird's-Foot Trefoil* shows;
This is my name which grown-ups use,
But children may call me what they choose.

◆ THE SONG OF ◆
THE NIGHTSHADE FAIRY

My name is Nightshade, also Bittersweet;
    Ah, little folk, be wise!
Hide you your hands behind you when we meet,
    Turn you away your eyes.
My flowers you shall not pick, nor berries eat,
    For in them poison lies.

(Though this is so poisonous, it is not the Deadly Nightshade,
but the Woody Nightshade. The berries turn red a little later on.)

The Nightshade Fairy

The Heather Fairy

◆ THE SONG OF ◆
THE HEATHER FAIRY

"Ho, Heather, ho! From south to north
Spread now your royal purple forth!
Ho, jolly one! From east to west,
The moorland waiteth to be dressed!"

I come, I come! With footsteps sure
I run to clothe the waiting moor;
From heath to heath I leap and stride
To fling my bounty far and wide.

(The heather in the picture is bell heather, or heath; it is
different from the common heather which is also called ling.)

◆ THE SONG OF ◆
THE SCARLET PIMPERNEL FAIRY

By the furrowed fields I lie,
Calling to the passers-by:
"If the weather you would tell,
Look at Scarlet Pimpernel."

When the day is warm and fine,
I unfold these flowers of mine;
Ah, but you must look for rain
When I shut them up again!

Weather-glasses on the walls
Hang in wealthy people's halls:
Though I lie where cart-wheels pass
I'm the Poor Man's Weather-Glass!

The Scarlet Pimpernel Fairy

The Greater Knapweed Fairy

◆ THE SONG OF ◆
THE GREATER KNAPWEED FAIRY

Oh, please, little children, take note of my
    name:
To call me a thistle is really a shame:
I'm harmless old Knapweed, who grows
    on the chalk,
I never will prick you when out for your
    walk.

Yet I should be sorry, yes, sorry indeed,
To cut your small fingers and cause them
    to bleed;
So bid me Good Morning when out for
    your walk,
And mind how you pull at my very tough
    stalk.

(Sometimes this Knapweed is called Hardhead; and he has a
brother, the little Knapweed, whose flower is not quite like this.)

159

◆ THE SONG OF ◆
THE ROSE FAIRY

Best and dearest flower that grows,
Perfect both to see and smell;
Words can never, never tell
Half the beauty of a Rose—
Buds that open to disclose
Fold on fold of purest white,
Lovely pink, or red that glows
Deep, sweet-scented. What delight
  To be Fairy of the Rose!

The Rose Fairy

The Michaelmas Daisy Fairy

◆ THE SONG OF ◆
THE MICHAELMAS DAISY FAIRY

"Red Admiral, Red Admiral,
   I'm glad to see you here,
     Alighting on my daisies one by one!
I hope you like their flavour
   and although the Autumn's near,
     Are happy as you sit there in the sun?"

"I thank you very kindly, sir!
   Your daisies *are* so nice,
     So pretty and so plentiful are they;
The flavour of their honey, sir,
   it really does entice;
     I'd like to bring my brothers, if I may!"

"Friend butterfly, friend butterfly,
   go fetch them one and all!
     I'm waiting here to welcome every guest;
And tell them it is Michaelmas,
   and soon the leaves will fall,
     But *I* think Autumn sunshine is the best!"

163

◆ THE SONG OF ◆
THE WAYFARING TREE FAIRY

My shoots are tipped with buds as dusty-grey
As ancient pilgrims toiling on their way.

Like Thursday's child with far to go, I stand,
All ready for the road to Fairyland;

With hood, and bag, and shoes, my name to suit,
And in my hand my gorgeous-tinted fruit.

The Wayfaring Tree Fairy

The Robin's Pincushion Fairy

◆ THE SONG OF ◆
THE ROBIN'S PINCUSHION FAIRY

People come and look at me,
Asking who this rogue may be?
—Up to mischief, they suppose,
Perched upon the briar-rose.

I am nothing else at all
But a fuzzy-wuzzy ball,
Like a little bunch of flame;
I will tell you how I came:

First there came a naughty fly,
Pricked the rose, and made her cry;
Out I popped to see about it;
This is true, so do not doubt it!

◆ THE SONG OF ◆
THE ACORN FAIRY

To English folk the mighty oak
　　Is England's noblest tree;
Its hard-grained wood is strong and good
　　As English hearts can be.
And would you know how oak-trees grow,
　　The secret may be told:
You do but need to plant for seed
　　One acorn in the mould;
For even so, long years ago,
　　Were born the oaks of old.

The Acorn Fairy

The Black Bryony Fairy

◆ THE SONG OF ◆
THE BLACK BRYONY FAIRY

Bright and wild and beautiful
For the Autumn festival,
I will hang from tree to tree
Wreaths and ropes of Bryony,
To the glory and the praise
Of the sweet September days.

(There is nothing black to be seen about this Bryony, but
people do say it has a black root; and this may be true, but you
would need to dig it up to find out. It used to be thought a cure
for freckles.)

◆ THE SONG OF ◆
THE BLACKBERRY FAIRY

My berries cluster black and thick
For rich and poor alike to pick.

I'll tear your dress, and cling, and tease,
And scratch your hands and arms and knees.

I'll stain your fingers and your face,
And then I'll laugh at your disgrace.

But when the bramble-jelly's made,
You'll find your trouble well repaid.

The Blackberry Fairy

The Rose Hip Fairy

◆ THE SONG OF ◆
THE ROSE HIP FAIRY

Cool dewy morning,
   Blue sky at noon,
White mist at evening,
   And large yellow moon;

Blackberries juicy
   For staining of lips;
And scarlet, O scarlet
   The Wild Rose Hips!

Gay as a gipsy
   All Autumn long,
Here on the hedge-top
   This is my song.

◆ THE SONG OF ◆
THE WHITE BRYONY FAIRY

Have you seen at Autumn-time
   Fairy-folk adorning
All the hedge with necklaces,
   Early in the morning?
Green beads and red beads
   Threaded on a vine:
Is there any handiwork
   Prettier than mine?

(This Bryony has other names—White Vine, Wild Vine, and
Red-berried Bryony. It has tendrils to climb with, which Black
Bryony has not, and its leaves and berries are quite different.
They say its root is white, as the other's is black.)

The White Bryony Fairy

The Beechnut Fairy

◆ THE SONG OF ◆
THE BEECHNUT FAIRY

O the great and happy Beech,
   Glorious and tall!
Changing with the changing months,
   Lovely in them all:

Lovely in the leafless time,
   Lovelier in green;
Loveliest with golden leaves
   And the sky between,

When the nuts are falling fast,
   Thrown by little me—
Tiny things to patter down
   From a forest tree!

(You may eat these.)

◆ THE SONG OF ◆
THE SNOWDROP FAIRY

Deep sleeps the Winter,
   Cold, wet, and grey;
Surely all the world is dead;
   Spring is far away.
Wait! the world shall waken;
   It is not dead, for lo,
The Fair Maids of February
   Stand in the snow!

The Snowdrop Fairy

The Spindle Berry Fairy

◆ THE SONG OF ◆
THE SPINDLE BERRY FAIRY

See the rosy-berried Spindle
All to sunset colours turning,
Till the thicket seems to kindle,
Just as though the trees were burning.
While my berries split and show
Orange-coloured seeds aglow,
One by one my leaves must fall:
Soon the wind will take them all.
Soon must fairies shut their eyes
For the Winter's hushabies;
But, before the Autumn goes,
Spindle turns to flame and rose!

◆ THE SONG OF ◆
THE PLANE TREE FAIRY

You will not find him in the wood,
    Nor in the country lane;
But in the city's parks and streets
    You'll see the Plane.

O turn your eyes from pavements grey,
    And look you up instead,
To where the Plane tree's pretty balls
    Hang overhead!

When he has shed his golden leaves,
    His balls will yet remain,
To deck the tree until the Spring
    Comes back again!

The Plane Tree Fairy

The Box Tree Fairy

◆ THE SONG OF ◆
THE BOX TREE FAIRY

Have you seen the Box unclipped,
Never shaped and never snipped?
Often it's a garden hedge,
Just a narrow little edge;
Or in funny shapes it's cut,
And it's very pretty; *but*—

But, unclipped, it is a tree,
Growing as it likes to be;
And it has its blossoms too;
Tiny buds, the Winter through,
Wait to open in the Spring
In a scented yellow ring.

And among its leaves there play
Little blue-tits, brisk and gay.

◆ THE SONG OF ◆
THE OLD-MAN'S-BEARD FAIRY

This is where the little elves
Cuddle down to hide themselves;
Into fluffy beds they creep,
Say good-night, and go to sleep.

(Old-Man's-Beard is Wild Clematis; its flowers are called
Traveller's Joy. This silky fluff belongs to the seeds.)

The Old-Man's-Beard Fairy

The Blackthorn Fairy

◆ THE SONG OF ◆
THE BLACKTHORN FAIRY

The wind is cold, the Spring seems long
   a-waking;
   The woods are brown and bare;
Yet this is March: soon April will be making
   All things most sweet and fair.

See, even now, in hedge and thicket tangled,
   One brave and cheering sight:
The leafless branches of the Blackthorn,
   spangled
   With starry blossoms white!

(The cold days of March are sometimes called "Blackthorn
Winter".)

◆ THE SONG OF ◆
THE WINTER ACONITE FAIRY

Deep in the earth
I woke, I stirred.
I said: "Was that the Spring I heard?
For something called!"
"No, no," they said;
"Go back to sleep. Go back to bed.

"You're far too soon;
The world's too cold
For you, so small." So I was told.
But how could I
Go back to sleep?
I could not wait; I had to peep!

Up, up, I climbed,
And here am I.
How wide the earth! How great the sky!
O wintry world,
See me, awake!
Spring calls, and comes; 'tis no mistake.

The Winter Aconite Fairy

The Christmas Tree Fairy

◆ THE SONG OF ◆
THE CHRISTMAS TREE FAIRY

The little Christmas Tree was born
    And dwelt in open air;
It did not guess how bright a dress
    Some day its boughs would wear;
Brown cones were all, it thought, a tall
    And grown-up Fir would bear.

O little Fir! Your forest home
    Is far and far away;
And here indoors these boughs of yours
    With coloured balls are gay,
With candle-light, and tinsel bright,
    For this is Christmas Day!

A dolly-fairy stands on top,
    Till children sleep; then she
(A live one now!) from bough to bough
    Goes gliding silently.
O magic sight, this joyous night!
    O laden, sparkling tree!

◆ THE SONG OF ◆
THE ROSE-BAY
WILLOW-HERB FAIRY

On the breeze my fluff is blown;
So my airy seeds are sown.

Where the earth is burnt and sad,
I will come to make it glad.

All forlorn and ruined places,
All neglected empty spaces,

I can cover—only think!—
With a mass of rosy pink.

Burst then, seed-pods; breezes, blow!
Far and wide my seeds shall go!

(Another name for this Willow-Herb is "Fireweed",
because of its way of growing where there have
been heath or forest fires.)

The Rose-Bay Willow-Herb Fairy

The Red Clover Fairy

◆ THE SONG OF ◆
THE RED CLOVER FAIRY

The Fairy: O, what a great big bee
Has come to visit me!
He's come to find my honey.
O, what a great big bee!

The Bee: O, what a great big Clover!
I'll search it well, all over,
And gather all its honey.
O, what a great big Clover!

199

◆ THE SONG OF ◆
THE TANSY FAIRY

In busy kitchens, in olden days,
Tansy was used in a score of ways;
Chopped and pounded,
    when cooks would make
Tansy puddings and tansy cake,
Tansy posset, or tansy tea;
Physic or flavouring tansy'd be.
        People who know
        Have told me so!

That is my tale of the past; today,
Still I'm here by the King's Highway,
Where the air from the fields
    is fresh and sweet,
With my fine-cut leaves and my flowers neat.
Were ever such button-like flowers seen—
Yellow, for elfin coats of green?
        Three in a row—
        I stitch them so!

200

The Tansy Fairy

The Agrimony Fairies

◆ THE SONG OF ◆
THE AGRIMONY FAIRIES

Spikes of yellow flowers,
　　All along the lane;
When the petals vanish,
　　Burrs of red remain.

First the spike of flowers,
　　Then the spike of burrs;
Carry them like soldiers,
　　Smartly, little sirs!

◆ THE SONG OF ◆
THE ALMOND BLOSSOM FAIRY

Joy! the Winter's nearly gone!
Soon will Spring come dancing on;
And, before her, here dance I,
Pink like sunrise in the sky.
Other lovely things will follow;
Soon will cuckoo come, and swallow;
Birds will sing and buds will burst,
But the Almond is the first!

The Almond Blossom Fairy

The Pear Blossom Fairy

◆ THE SONG OF ◆
THE PEAR BLOSSOM FAIRY

Sing, sing, sing, you blackbirds!
　Sing, you beautiful thrush!
It's Spring, Spring, Spring; so sing, sing, sing,
　From dawn till the stars say "hush".

See, see, see the blossom
　On the Pear Tree shining white!
It will fall like snow, but the pears will grow
　For people's and birds' delight.

Build, build, build, you chaffinch;
　Build, you robin and wren,
A safe warm nest where your eggs may rest;
　Then sit, sit, sit, little hen!

◆ THE SONG OF ◆
THE LILAC FAIRY

White May is flowering,
  Red May beside;
Laburnum is showering
  Gold far and wide;
But *I* sing of Lilac,
  The dearly-loved Lilac,
Lilac, in Maytime
  A joy and a pride!

I love her so much
  That I never can tell
If she's sweeter to look at,
  Or sweeter to smell.

The Lilac Fairy

The Beech Tree Fairy

◆ THE SONG OF ◆
THE BEECH TREE FAIRY

The trunks of Beeches are smooth and grey,
 Like tall straight pillars of stone
In great Cathedrals where people pray;
 Yet from tiny things they've grown.
About their roots is the moss; and wide
 Their branches spread, and high;
It seems to us, on the earth who bide,
 That their heads are in the sky.

And when Spring is here,
 and their leaves appear,
  With a silky fringe on each,
Nothing is seen so new and green
 As the new young green of Beech.
O the great grey Beech is young, is young,
 When, dangling soft and small,
Round balls of bloom from its twigs are hung,
 And the sun shines over all.

211

◆ THE SONG OF ◆
THE GUELDER ROSE FAIRIES

There are two little trees:
In the garden there grows
The one with the snowballs;
All children love *those*!

The other small tree
Not everyone knows,
With her blossoms spread flat—
Yet they're both Guelder Rose!

But the garden Guelder has nothing
    When her beautiful balls are shed;
While in Autumn her wild little sister
    Bears berries of ruby red!

The Guelder Rose Fairies

The Elder Fairy

◆ THE SONG OF ◆
THE ELDER FAIRY

When the days have grown in length,
When the sun has greater power,
Shining in his noonday strength;
When the Elder Tree's in flower;
When each shady kind of place
By the stream and up the lane,
Shows its mass of creamy lace—
Summer's really come again!

◆ THE SONG OF ◆
THE CHERRY TREE FAIRY

Cherries, a treat for the blackbirds;
    Cherries for girls and boys;
And there's never an elf in the treetops
    But cherries are what he enjoys!

Cherries in garden and orchard,
    Ripe and red in the sun;
And the merriest elf in the treetops
    Is the fortunate Cherry-tree one!

The Cherry Tree Fairy

The Poplar Fairy

◆ THE SONG OF ◆
THE POPLAR FAIRY

White fluff is drifting like snow round our feet;
    Puff! it goes blowing
    Away down the street.

Where does it come from? Look up and see!
    There, from the Poplar!
    Yes, from that tree!

Tassels of silky white fluffiness there
    Hang among leaves
    All a-shake in the air.

Fairies, you well may guess, use it to stuff
    Pillows and cushions,
    And play with it—puff!

(This is called the Black Poplar; but only, I think, because
there is also a White Poplar, which has white leaves. The
very tall thin Poplar is the Lombardy.)

219

◆ THE SONG OF ◆
THE ELM TREE FAIRY

Soft and brown in Winter-time,
Dark and green in Summer's prime,
All their leaves a yellow haze
In the pleasant Autumn days—
See the lines of Elm trees stand
Keeping watch through all the land
Over lanes, and crops, and cows,
And the fields where Dobbin ploughs.
All day long, with listening ears,
Sits the Elm-tree Elf, and hears
Distant bell, and bleat, and bark,
Whistling boy, and singing lark.
Often on the topmost boughs
Many a rook has built a house;
Evening comes; and overhead,
Cawing, home they fly to bed.

The Elm Tree Fairy

The Scilla Fairy

◆ THE SONG OF ◆
THE SCILLA FAIRY

"Scilla, Scilla, tell me true,
Why are you so very blue?"

Oh, I really cannot say
Why I'm made this lovely way!

I might know, if I were wise.
Yet—I've heard of seas and skies,

Where the blue is deeper far
Than our skies of Springtime are.

P'r'aps I'm here to let you see
What that Summer blue will be.

When you see it, think of me!

◆ THE SONG OF ◆
THE FORGET-ME-NOT FAIRY

Where do fairy babies lie
Till they're old enough to fly?
Here's a likely place, I think,
'Mid these flowers, blue and pink,
(Pink for girls and blue for boys:
Pretty things for babies' toys!)
Let us peep now, gently. Why,
Fairy baby, here you lie!

Kicking there, with no one by,
Baby dear, how good you lie!
All alone, but O, you're not—
You could *never* be—forgot!
O how glad I am I've found you,
With Forget-me-nots around you,
Blue, the colour of the sky!
Fairy baby, Hushaby!

The Forget-me-not Fairy

The Tulip Fairy

◆ THE SONG OF ◆
THE TULIP FAIRY

Our stalks are very straight and tall,
    Our colours clear and bright;
Too many-hued to name them all—
    Red, yellow, pink, or white.

And some are splashed, and some, maybe,
    As dark as any plum.
From tulip-fields across the sea
    To England did we come.

We were a peaceful country's pride,
    And Holland is its name.
Now in your gardens we abide—
    And aren't you glad we came?

(But long, long ago, tulips were brought from Persian
gardens, before there were any in Holland.)

227

◆ THE SONG OF ◆
THE PINK FAIRIES

Early in the mornings,
   when children still are sleeping,
Or late, late at night-time,
   beneath the summer moon,
What are they doing,
   the busy fairy people?
Could you creep to spy them,
   in silent magic shoon,

You might learn a secret,
   among the garden borders,
Something never guessed at,
   that no one knows or thinks:
Snip, snip, snip, go busy fairy scissors,
Pinking out the edges
   of the petals of the Pinks!

Pink Pinks, white Pinks,
   double Pinks, and single,—
Look at them and see
   if it's not the truth I tell!
Why call them Pinks
   if they weren't pinked out by *someone*?
And what but fairy scissors
   could pink them out so well?

The Pink Fairies

The Snapdragon Fairy

◆ THE SONG OF ◆
THE SNAPDRAGON FAIRY

Into the Dragon's mouth he goes;
  Never afraid is he!
There's honey within for him, he knows,
  Clever old Bumble Bee!
The mouth snaps tight; he is lost to sight—
  How will he ever get out?
He's doing it backwards—nimbly too,
  Though he is somewhat stout!

Off to another mouth he goes;
  Never a rest has he;
He must fill his honey-bag full, he knows—
  Busy old Bumble Bee!
And Snapdragon's name is only a game—
  It isn't as fierce as it sounds;
The Snapdragon Elf is pleased as Punch
  When Bumble comes on his rounds!

◆ THE SONG OF ◆
THE LAVENDER FAIRY

"Lavender's blue, diddle diddle"—
    So goes the song;
All round her bush, diddle diddle,
    Butterflies throng;
(They love her well, diddle diddle,
    So do the bees;)
While she herself, diddle diddle,
    Sways in the breeze!

"Lavender's blue, diddle diddle,
    Lavender's green";
She'll scent the clothes, diddle diddle,
    Put away clean—
Clean from the wash, diddle diddle,
    Hanky and sheet;
Lavender's spikes, diddle diddle,
    Make them all sweet!

(The word "blue" was often used in old days where
we should say "purple" or "mauve".)

The Lavender Fairy

The Heliotrope Fairy

◆ THE SONG OF ◆
THE HELIOTROPE FAIRY

Heliotrope's my name; and why
People call me "Cherry Pie",
That I really do not know;
But perhaps they call me so,
'Cause I give them such a treat,
Just like something nice to eat.
For my scent—O come and smell it!
How can words describe or tell it?
And my buds and flowers, see,
Soft and rich and velvety—
Deepest purple first, that fades
To the palest lilac shades.
Well-beloved, I know, am I—
Heliotrope, or Cherry Pie!

◆ THE SONG OF ◆
THE MARIGOLD FAIRY

Great Sun above me in the sky,
So golden, glorious, and high,
My petals, see, are golden too;
They shine, but cannot shine like you.

I scatter many seeds around;
And where they fall upon the ground,
More Marigolds will spring, more flowers
To open wide in sunny hours.

It is because I love you so,
I turn to watch you as you go;
Without your light, no joy could be.
Look down, great Sun, and shine on me!

The Marigold Fairy

Bugle

The Bugle Fairy

♦ THE SONG OF ♦
THE BUGLE FAIRY

At the edge of the woodland
Where good fairies dwell,
Stands, on the look-out,
A brave sentinel.

At the call of his bugle
Out the elves run,
Ready for anything,
Danger, or fun,
Hunting, or warfare,
By moonshine or sun.

With bluebells and campions
The woodlands are gay,
Where bronzy-leaved Bugle
Keeps watch night and day.

◆ THE SONG OF ◆
THE DOUBLE DAISY FAIRY

Dahlias and Delphiniums,
  you're too tall for me;
Isn't there a *little* flower
  I can choose for D?

In the smallest flower-bed
Double Daisy lifts his head,
With a smile to greet the sun,
You, and me, and everyone.

Crimson Daisy, now I see
You're the little lad for me!

Double Daisy

The Double Daisy Fairy

Gorse

The Gorse Fairies

◆ THE SONG OF ◆
THE GORSE FAIRIES

"When gorse is out of blossom,"
   (Its prickles bare of gold)
"Then kissing's out of fashion,"
   Said country-folk of old.
Now Gorse is in its glory
   In May when skies are blue,
But when its time is over,
   Whatever shall we do?

O dreary would the world be,
   With everyone grown cold—
Forlorn as prickly bushes
   Without their fairy gold!
But this will never happen:
   At every time of year
You'll find one bit of blossom—
   A kiss from someone dear!

◆ THE SONG OF ◆
THE LILY-OF-THE-VALLEY FAIRY

Gentle fairies, hush your singing:
Can you hear my white bells ringing,
Ringing as from far away?
Who can tell me what they say?

Little snowy bells out-springing
From the stem and softly ringing—
Tell they of a country where
Everything is good and fair?

Lovely, lovely things for L!
Lilac, Lavender as well;
And, more sweet than rhyming tells,
Lily-of-the-Valley's bells.

(Lily-of-the-Valley is sometimes called Ladders to Heaven.)

Lily-of-the-Valley

The Lily-of-the-Valley Fairy

Queen of the Meadow

The Queen of the Meadow Fairy

◆ THE SONG OF ◆
THE QUEEN OF THE MEADOW FAIRY

Queen of the Meadow
    where small streams are flowing,
What is your kingdom
    and whom do you rule?
"Mine are the places
    where wet grass is growing,
Mine are the people
    of marshland and pool.

"Kingfisher-courtiers,
    swift-flashing, beautiful,
Dragon-flies, minnows,
    are mine one and all;
Little frog-servants who
    wait round me, dutiful,
Hop on my errands
    and come when I call."

Gentle Queen Meadowsweet,
    served with such loyalty,
Have you no crown then,
    no jewels to wear?
"Nothing I need
    for a sign of my royalty,
Nothing at all
    but my own fluffy hair!"

◆ THE SONG OF ◆
THE STRAWBERRY FAIRY

A flower for S!
Is Sunflower he?
He's handsome, yes,
But what of me?—

In my party suit
Of red and white,
And a gift of fruit
For the feast tonight:

Strawberries small
And wild and sweet,
For the Queen and all
Of her Court to eat!

Strawberry

The Strawberry Fairy

Wallflower

The Wallflower Fairy

◆ THE SONG OF ◆
THE WALLFLOWER FAIRY

Wallflower, Wallflower, up on the wall,
Who sowed your seed there?
              "No one at all:
Long, long ago it was blown by the breeze
To the crannies of walls
   where I live as I please.

"Garden walls, castle walls, mossy and old,
These are my dwellings;
   from these I behold
The changes of years;
   yet, each spring that goes by,
Unchanged in my sweet-smelling
   velvet am I!"

◆ THE SONG OF ◆
THE ZINNIA FAIRY

Z for Zinnias, pink or red;
See them in the flower-bed,
Copper, orange, all aglow,
Making such a stately show.

I, their fairy, say Good-bye,
For the last of all am I.
Now the Alphabet is said
All the way from A to Z.

Zinnia

The Zinnia Fairy